More Adventures In The Magic Cave

by

Aarti Gosine

JAV Publishing House Limited
22 Nelson Street
Perseverance
Couva
Trinidad, W.I.
javpublishing@gmail.com

Telephone: 1- 868 – 636- 0023
                  1- 868 - 681- 7308

Published in Trinidad and Tobago by JAV Publishing House Limited

© JAV Publishing House Limited 2011

ISBN   978-0-9847981-0-0

Illustrations: Joanne Boopsingh
Cover Design: Simone Rudder

1

Back to the Cave

It was the last day of the school term. With loud laughter and lots of chatter, Alan, Samantha and Mark bade farewell to their school. Two glorious months of freedom, and their cave awaited them. The children were exploding with anticipation as to what the cave had in store for them.

"Maybe we will go to another planet," Mark wondered.
"I would like to meet some cuddly polar bears," Samantha said.

"Polar bears? They are dangerous and not cuddly," Alan said to his sister.

"Well maybe a deserted island then. Like in the book we were reading in class."

"It doesn't matter," said Alan, the voice of reason. "The cave will be whatever it wants to be."

"Ok. Well let's go and see what it is today," said Mark.

Alan and Samantha were twins who had recently moved to Vance Falls. Mark was their lanky best friend who lived nearby.

After moving to Vance Falls with their parents and meeting Mark, the three children discovered
a magic cave. The cave changed into different places each time they entered.

Since for the next two months they did not have to worry about studying or doing homework, they were eager to continue their adventures in the cave.

After changing into their play clothes, they raced towards their beloved cave, their hearts pounding with excitement. Within seconds they had removed the small rocks that blocked their squeeze-though entrance and pushed their way inside.

Stretching out before them was a dry, brown expanse of land as far as the eye could see. There were very few trees and most of the vegetation consisted of tufts of brown grass. The sun blazed down on them from the cloudless sky.

"It's so hot here!" exclaimed Samantha.
"What is this place?" asked Mark

"Look over there!" Samantha exclaimed pointing to a herd of zebras grazing in the distance.

"Zebras," said Alan moving closer towards the herd. "I know where this is. It's the savannahs of Africa."

"Africa? We're in Africa?"

"Yes. Remember we learnt about the Serengeti plains of Africa in school?"

"I remember. Maybe we are on a reserve? There might be more animals around."

"Let's not go too close to the zebras," Samantha cautioned. "We don't want to scare them."

The children turned away from the zebras and continued to explore their surroundings. They had learnt about the grasslands of Africa in their geography class at school. Their teacher was teaching them about the seven continents of the world and Africa was the first one that they studied.

In the distance they saw giraffes stretching their long necks to eat the leaves from the tall trees that dotted the landscape. The children crept through the grass, getting closer and closer to the tall creatures.

"Did you know that the giraffes are the tallest animals in the world?" Alan said. He loved all animals and was always reading books on them. He had a large collection of farm animals and zoo animals in his toy box.

"They are very tall. Almost as tall as a skyscraper," Mark commented.

In the meantime Samantha who was not listening to them crept even closer to the
giraffes. She also liked animals and thought that all of them were cute and cuddly. She did not realize that some animals were very dangerous and could kill her. Alan and Mark were so engrossed in their discussion about the giraffes that they did not notice that she was not with them anymore.

Suddenly they heard a scream. They jumped up from their crouched position in the grass and saw Samantha standing in front of a giraffe. It was lowering his head to get a better look at her.

"Stay still Sam," Alan called out to his sister.

"Otherwise he might eat you."

"Mark! Don't say that!"

"Serves her right. She is always bothering the animals."

The giraffe lowered his head and was curiously eying Samantha. He had never seen such a strange creature before. He craned his head from side to side and looked at her through his large, bulging eyes.

Samantha was frozen in terror. Her heart was pounding so much that her chest hurt.The nine hundred kilogram animal was staring at her straight in the face. The giraffe continued to look at her curiously and then suddenly he flicked out his long, black tongue and licked her!

"Ahh!" she screamed. "Somebody help me!"

"Don't be scared little one," the giraffe said and Samantha almost fainted. "I will not hurt you."

"You can talk?" she asked after she recovered from her shock.

"Of course I can talk. All the animals here could talk. What's your name? I am Ken, short for Kensignton."

"I…I… am Samantha. Nice to meet you Ken." She was still shivering in fear.

By this time Alan and Mark came running to save her as they thought the giraffe was going to harm her.

"Shoo! Shoo! Get away! Leave her alone!"

The giraffe raised his head and looked at these new creatures coming towards him. Alan ran straight up to the giraffe yelling at the top of his lungs. The giraffe merely looked at him.

"Could you not shout so loud!" the giraffe said.

The boys stopped in their tracks.

"Did you say that?" Alan asked the giraffe.

"Do you see anyone else around here?"

"Wow!" Mark exclaimed. "A talking giraffe!"

"Hey who are you talking to?" asked another voice.

The children peered around the giraffe to see a zebra standing behind him.

"Look! It's a zebra!" exclaimed Samantha.
"Yes. That's me. Marie is my name," the zebra said sauntering up to them.

"Are you a girl zebra? You look like you have lipstick on," said Samantha.

"Oh God! Don't get her started," Ken groaned.

"Oh! You like my lipstick?" asked Marie lowering her head so Samantha could see it better. "It's the berries from the holly bush. It's my favourite colour."

"So what are you kids doing here?" Ken asked them.

"We came through the entrance of a cave and ended up here," Mark tried to explain.

"Cave? I never saw any cave around here," Ken said frowning. "Are you sure?"
"Yes. We're sure!" Alan exclaimed a little offended.

"Never mind where they came from," said Marie. "Let's go down by the river. I'm thirsty and maybe Emmanuel will be there."

"You go ahead. I am still hungry and these leaves are delicious," Ken said eying the leaves on the tree close by.

"Who's Emmanuel?" Samantha asked Marie.

"Oh. He is my handsome boyfriend."

"Yeah right! You wish," Ken retorted.

"You're just jealous Ken," Marie replied sauntering off while Ken resumed chomping on the uppermost leaves of the tree.

The children raced off after Marie eager to meet other animals of the savannah.

"Look over there!" Samantha stopped abruptly and pointed to some ostriches almost hidden by the tall grass.

"Oh. You don't want to meet them," Marie told them.

"Why not?"

"They are even grumpier than Ken. Mean birds in my opinion."

The ostriches heard their voices and stopped feeding to look at them.

"What are you staring at?" the biggest one asked them. "Can't you see we're trying to eat? Marie, please take your friends and move along."

"Let's get out of here," said Alan. "They are mean."

"Told you," said Marie.

After a few minutes stroll, they arrived at the river. Stretching before them as far as the eye could see was the widest river they had ever encountered. They couldn't even see the opposite bank.

"This river is huge!"

"Yes. It is," Marie replied. "This is the Mara River and it runs through this animal reserve."

The kids were speechless. On the banks of the river, in the shallow muddy water there were several hippopotamuses cooling themselves. A little higher up there was a heard of zebras drinking and splashing in the water.

"Let's move higher up," Marie told them. "I want to see if Emmanuel is up there."

"Is Emmanuel really your boyfriend?" Samantha asked.
"Not yet. But soon." She winked at them.

They walked closer to the zebras that stopped what they were doing to look at them. Some of them whispered among themselves about the strange looking creatures.

"Hey it's not polite to whisper about people," Marie yelled at them.

All the whispering stopped. Apparently Marie had some rank in the heard.

"Look! There is Emmanuel," Marie said leading them over to a large, muscular and handsome zebra.

Emmanuel saw them approaching and came up to them.

"Hi Manny," Marie crooned batting her long eyelashes at him.

"Hi Marie. Who are your friends?"

Marie introduced the children to Emmanuel.

"I have never seen animals of your kind before but welcome to our part of river. Would you care to have a drink?"

"I am kinda thirsty," said Mark.

"Go right ahead then."

Mark stopped, confused.

"You have to drink from the river," Alan told him. "You thought they were going to bring it for you in a glass?"

Samantha and Alan laughed while Mark lowered his head and walked to the bank of the river. For a few minutes he looked at the muddy water and then walked back to the group.
"What happened?" Samantha asked him. "Not thirsty anymore?"

"No. I think I will wait until we get back home."

The sound of pounding hooves caught their attention. When they turned around, they saw a very angry looking zebra coming towards them.

"Oh oh! This looks like trouble," Alan whispered to Samantha.

"What's she doing here!" exclaimed Marie.

"Marie! Calm down," said Emmanuel.

"Emmanuel!" the new zebra exclaimed. "What are you doing talking to her?" she asked pointing towards Marie.

"Excuse me! Who do you think you are pointing to?" asked Marie angrily. It was obvious that she was not happy to see this new zebra.

"Abba," Emmanuel said stepping between the two ladies. "I can talk to whomsoever I want. I am the leader of this herd."

"But I am your girlfriend! And I don't like her," Abba replied.

"You are not his girlfriend. I am," said Marie pushing Abba away.

"Oh no! Looks like they are going to fight."

"Well you know the rules. If you both want me you will have to fight. Only one of you can be my girlfriend," Emmanuel told Marie and Abba.

"You are going to let them fight over you?" Alan asked Emmanuel.
"Yes. That's the only way this will be settled. They hate each other."

Although they didn't like the idea of Marie and Abba fighting, they had to accept that this was the way the zebras settled things.

Meanwhile, the two zebras were pushing and shoving each other. Both seemed equally matched. Suddenly Marie rose on her hind legs and jumped on Abba's back. Abba fell to the ground with Marie on top of her.

Marie continued to snap at Abba while she struggled to get up.

"Is Marie going to kill her?" Samantha asked scared.

"No. She just wants to frighten her."

Marie continued to snap and hit at Abba who was getting tired. Suddenly Marie jumped off and Abba jumped up and ran away.

"See. She was no match for me," Marie panted as she came to stand at Emmanuel's side.

"No. She wasn't my dear," said Emmanuel nuzzling Marie. "She wasn't strong enough to be the girlfriend of the herd leader. But you are."

"Are you ok?" Marie asked the children. "I am sorry you had to see that but that's how we settle disputes."

"We're ok," Alan replied although they were still stunned by what they saw. "But I think it's time for us to go home."

Emmanuel and Marie walked the children back to the mouth of the cave. Along the way they showed them a pride of lions playing with their cubs.

"Aww! They are so cute!" Samantha exclaimed. "Can I play with them?"

"No my dear," Emmanuel said. "Mother lionesses are very protective of their cubs just like humans are of their young."

"Go ahead Sam. She might eat you!" Mark teased her.

"It's ok. I can just look at them from here."

The children enjoyed looking at the chubby cubs play with each other, rolling and tumbling in the dust. They even attempted to tug at their father's long mane but he gently growled at them.

After a few minutes the twins and Mark bade Marie and Emmanuel goodbye and left for home.

"What an interesting day!" Mark exclaimed.
"Yes. We learnt a lot about life on the savannahs."

"I wonder if two girls will fight for me like Marie and Abba?" Mark asked.

"I doubt it very much," Alan replied grinning at his friend.

2

Shoes, Shoes, Shoes

Anya did not want her children to waste their two months' vacation. Instead she enrolled them and Mark in a summer camp at the local YMCA. Although the kids enjoyed the activities at the camp, nothing could compare to their adventures inside the cave.

As soon as camp was finished for the day they would run to the cave, hearts pounding in anticipation. Today was no different.

Stepping inside, they were greeted by the noise of hammers on iron and of pounding footsteps.

"What's going on in here?" Samantha asked as they waited for their eyes to adjust to the dimness of the cave.

"I don't know but sounds like they are making something."

Soon they recognized a few tiny creatures about one foot tall rushing about the cave. The 'creatures' were wearing tights, boots, stripped tops and pointed hats.

"They're elves!" Samantha exclaimed as the children ventured further inside.

"Yes. And they are making shoes," Mark replied as he left the twins and went closer to the elves.

There were about one hundred elves scurrying around the place. Some were cutting leather, others were attaching the soles to the shoes and the rest were polishing and shining the finished product.

"Excuse me! Excuse me!" exclaimed one elf bustling by Mark. "Can't you see you are in the way?"

The elf hurried off before Mark could reply. Soon another one came running by. Mark gently picked him up by his waist.

"Hey, put me down!" the little elf yelled. "Put me down, you big oaf!"

"Who are you calling an oaf? Would you like it if I don't put you down?"

"Put me down now!" The elf started kicking at Mark, his two legs flaying out beneath him.

"Come on Mark. Put him down. You are scaring him," Samantha said.

"Yes put me down! Put me down!" The elf started to struggle and Mark had no choice but to put him down.

However, he did not run away but stared at Samantha. "You are very pretty. What are you? You are not an elf."

Samantha kneeled down to get closer to him. "My name is Samantha and I am a girl."

"A girl? Never met a 'girl' before but you are pretty."

"Thank you," Samantha said blushing. "What is your name?"

"I'm Ronald," the elf replied holding out his hand to her. "Nice to meet you Ronald," Samantha said shaking his tiny hand.

At that same time Alan joined the group and Ronald jumped back startled.

"Oh no! It's another oaf!"

"I am not an oaf," Alan told him, kneeling down to be closer to Ronald. "I am Samantha's brother, Alan."

"Nice to meet you, Alan. But you are not as pretty as Samantha," Ronald told him looking up at Samantha with stars in his eyes.

"So what is this place?" Alan asked.

"This is where all the shoes in the world are made." Ronald told them waving his hands proudly around the cave.

"All the shoes in the world! Wow! That's a lot of shoes."

"Yes. It's a lot of work too because humans can't seem to have enough shoes. They are always buying and buying even though the old ones are still good. And the orders keep coming in for more and more."

"I like shoes," Samantha told him. "Especially ones with little flowers on them."

"We make all sorts of shoes here. High heels, boots, flats, sneakers, hiking boots, football boots and even enchanted boots."

"Enchanted boots?" all three children asked in unison.

"Yes, enchanted boots. Come and see but you have to promise not to tell anyone."

"We promise," Samantha told him. "No one will believe us anyway."

Ronald led them across the work floor, past elves so busy working on their shoes that they did not even notice the giants walking among them. To the back of the work area was a large, heavy wooden door. However there were no locks or handles on the door.

"How do you open it?" Mark asked.

"With magic of course."

Ronald took a small cloth bag from his pocket and retrieved some powder from it. This he gently blew on the door.

"So anyone who has that powder can open the door? Mark asked. "That's not very secure."

"No silly oaf. We're smarter than that. An elf has to blow on it for it to work. So only elves can open the door."

As the heavy door finally swung open, the children gasped at what they saw.

Along each wall were rows and rows of new, spotless glowing shoes.

"Wow! They're so pretty." Samantha marveled as she walked along the rows.

"I like this one and this one and this one…."

'I am sure you like all," her brother cut her off. "Why are these shoes so special?"

"They each give the wearer a special quality like making him look prettier, or play a sport better or make him invisible."

"Invisible? Wow! Invisible!" Mark said intrigued. "Which ones are they?"

"I…ah..am…I really shouldn't tell you. I should not have even brought you in here. If the bosses find out I will get in trouble."

"Oh, just a little peak. What harm could it cause?"

"Please Ronald," Samantha pleaded. She was also intrigued by shoes that can make you invisible.

'Just a little peak." He climbed up the ladder and from the uppermost shelf retrieved a pair of ordinary looking black boots.

"That's the magic shoes!" Alan exclaimed. "They look like a pair of regular Wellingtons."
"Well they have to look like normal shoes so that people won't get suspicious," Ronald told them defending the boots.

"He has a point there," Alan said.

"I don't think they are special. I think you are just fooling us," Mark said to the elf.

"They are special! They are magical boots!" Ronald exclaimed stamping his feet on the ground.

"How can we know for sure? They just look like rubber boots. I think you are just fooling us."

"I am not fooling you. Try it on and see for yourself."

That was exactly what Mark was waiting to hear. He grabbed the boots from Ronald's hand and slipped them over his sneakers. Samantha and Alan stared at him. He was starting to disappear beginning from his feet.

"Look! Alan! He is disappearing! He is turning invisible!" Samantha exclaimed excitedly.

Slowly but surely, Mark was starting to fade before their eyes.

"Oh my! My feet are gone! And now my belly and shoulders and hands!"

Soon enough all they could see was Mark's head which seemed to be floating in air. In seconds that too was gone and he had turned completely invisible.

"Mark! Mark! Where are you?" Samantha asked.

"Over here," said a voice close to the door.

"No! Don't go out the door!" Ronald exclaimed running towards the voice. "I will get in serious trouble."

But Mark did not hear him. He was already out on the work floor running among the busy elves.

Alan and Samantha ran after him. They did not realize that he would run out the door with the shoes on. They had to catch him before Ronald got in serious trouble with the older elves.

"Ouch! Hey! What's going on?" They could hear the working elves shout and some of them went tumbling on the floor.

"Who hit me?" another one asked.

"Hey, put me down!" they heard the yelling and when they turned to him they could only see an elf dangling in the air.

"Bam!" Some of the equipment got knocked over and half-made shoes were strewn about the floor.

"We have to stop him! He is creating havoc!" Alan yelled to Samantha.

"Oh my dear! Oh my dear! I am going to get in big trouble," Ronald said on the verge of tears.

Samantha knelt and gave the little elf a hug. "Don't worry Ronald. We will catch him and everything will be ok."

Ronald wiped his tears away with his little handkerchief and looked up at her. "I hope so," he said through his sniffles.

Alan and Samantha discussed how they were going to catch Mark. Since they could not see him it did not make sense to chase him.

"We have to trip him and make him fall. Then we could jump on him," Samantha said.

"Good idea, Sam." Alan beamed at his sister. "Now if the elves could help us, we could run wires across his path and that would make him fall."

"Yes. And then we could jump on him and take off the boots."
With Ronald's help, the twins organized the elves into groups and placed them at strategic locations on the work floor. They ran fine wires across the walk way and hoped for the best.

Mark was still up to no good. He had knocked over the shelves of newly-made shoes. He was also picking up the elves and holding them in mid-air while they kicked and yelled to be put down.

"We have to get him to come in this direction," Alan told Samantha and Ronald.

"Leave it to me," Ronald said as he ran to the middle of the floor. "Hey, you big oaf! Come and get me! Stop picking on those elves!"

An eerie silence filled the air. Nothing was falling and crashing and all the elves, except for Ronald, were silent.

"Over here!" he continued to yell, waving his arms in the air.

His small voice was no more than a squeak but in the silent tavern it could be heard loud and clear.

Suddenly the floor began to shake and a rumbling sound filled the air. Mark was on the move and running towards Ronald. As the footsteps came closer and closer, the elves pulled the wire even tighter and Samantha and Alan prepared to pounce on Mark and pull off the magical shoes.

Closer and closer he came and with a loud scream and crash fell to the ground. Immediately Alan fell on where he thought Mark's invisible body might be and held him down. Samantha, Ronald and some of the elves ran to his feet and started feeling around for the boots.
"Get off me! Leave me alone!" Mark roared at them.

Alan struggled to keep him pinned to the ground while Samantha and the elves took off his boots, which was no easy task as he kept kicking at them. Finally, they were able to pull both sides off.

"Look! He is starting to show again!" Samantha exclaimed as the top of Mark's head started appearing.

Alan let go of him and as he lay panting on the floor from the struggle. Now his entire body became visible.

"What happened?" he asked as he looked around him dazed.

"What happened!" Alan exclaimed angrily. "You tricked Ronald and put on the magic shoes and then created havoc out here!"

"I didn't mean to," Mark said lowering his head in shame. "I don't know what came over me."

"Well we don't believe you," Samantha told him. "Because of you Ronald will get in big trouble and all these lovely shoes are damaged."

"I am sorry. I didn't mean to."

"You should apologize to the elves."

However as Mark stood up to apologize to them they all turned their backs to him. They were furious and an apology was not going to satisfy them.

"I think you should just leave," Ronald told them in a low voice.

Samantha, who really liked the elf, was sad to see how hurt he was. They bade him a quiet goodbye and left the cave.

On the way home neither Alan nor Samantha spoke to Mark. They were both very sad about what happened to the elves.

3

Strange Goings On

After the incident with the elves, the twins did not see Mark for several days. He neither came to visit them nor did he come to the summer camp. The twins, at first, did not want to see him. They felt badly about what happened and also felt responsible for the damage that Mark caused.

For several days their interest in anything was low. They went to camp and then occupied themselves around the house. They had no desire to go back to the cave immediately.

About two nights after the incident, a loud 'thud' jolted Alan out of his sleep.

"Who's there?" he asked looking around his dark room.

There was no response. His heart started to beat faster.

"I know someone is there. Sam, is that you?"

No response. Suddenly the door to his room closed. Alan scrambled off his bed and flicked on the lights. The room was empty. His racing heart started to slow down. He listened carefully but all he could hear were the regular night sounds. Maybe he was just dreaming, he said to himself.

The next day he asked Samantha if she had heard anything since their rooms were adjacent. She said that she had slept peacefully throughout the night.

Later that day he asked her, "Sam did you move my book from the coffee table?" Alan was an avid reader.

"What book? The one about aliens? No I didn't move it. I haven't seen it."

"Strange," he muttered moving all the cushions from the chairs to see if it was under them. "I could swear I left it on this table."

He asked his parents if they saw his book but neither of them knew where it was.
The day wore on without any sign of the book. After searching all the obvious places, Alan gave up and started to read another book.

That night Anya made a special dinner for her children. Like most mothers she insisted that they eat healthy but she knew that the twins did not particularly like greens and vegetables. Dinner was baked chicken, baked potatoes, macaroni pie and sweet corn. There was nothing green on the menu.

"Oh, mom! This looks great!" Samantha exclaimed.

"Yummy! And no vegetables!"

"Enjoy it but don't get used to it. It's just for tonight." Anya smiled at them.

The food was delicious and the twins even asked for seconds. Half way through the meal, Snoopy, the family's terrier, perked his eyes up and suddenly became alert.

"What is it Snoopy?" their dad asked. "What are you hearing boy?"

He bounded out of the room and stood at the foot of the stairs barking incessantly at something upstairs. Alan and Samantha ran after him.

"What is he barking at?" Samantha asked looking up the stairs but not daring to go up.

"I don't know but I could swear I heard footsteps running up the stairs."

"Footsteps? Are you sure? There is no one else here but us," Samantha said. "You are just trying to scare me."

By this time Snoopy had stopped his barking and had returned to the dinner table to beg for scraps for food. The twins heard nothing else and returned to their meal.

For the next few days the rain poured continuously. At nights it was comforting to hear the raindrops on the galvanize roof but the rain kept the children inside during the day.

However, they were not bored. Strange things continued to go on inside the Harris' home. Alan's books disappeared and re-appeared in strange places and the pieces of their chess set were moved around. They continued to hear tiny footsteps around the house but couldn't find any animals in the house except Snoopy.

"Sam! Why did you eat half of my cake?" Alan yelled at his sister.

"I didn't eat your cake. I was taking a shower." Samantha had just walked into the room, her wet hair hanging limply around her shoulders.

"So then who ate my cake?"

"Not me!" She paused for a second. "Some weird things have been going on around the house. I wonder who is doing it."

"We have to set a trap to find out. I wonder if it is a ghost."

"A ghost, Sam? I don't think so but we should set a trap."

These strange things occurred when neither of them was in the room. As a result, they decided to put out some brownies and milk that night and hide and see what happened. They decided to do it in their bedroom, away from their parents' eyes.

Samantha was not too thrilled about a 'ghost' coming into their room but it was the only room in which they would not be bothered by their parents. That evening while their mom and dad were looking at the evening news, they sneaked two brownies and a glass of milk up to their room. If the 'ghost' liked cake, then he would surely like these double-chocolate brownies.

"How long do you think we will have to wait?" Samantha asked her brother.

"I don't know but we better take off the lights and pretend we are asleep."

They had set up their little experiment in Alan's room. They then both got into his bed, pulled up the covers and pretended to be asleep. With the rain softly drumming on the roof, the children were as snug as bugs in a rug.

They were about to drift off to sleep when they heard the bedroom door slowly open. It opened about two inches and then closed. Alan knew it was not his mother or father. He quietly nudged Samantha under the covers and put a finger to her lips so that she would know to be quiet.

He peered over the covers but couldn't see anything. They could, however, hear the soft shuffle of feet on the carpet. There was definitely something in the room!

Samantha heard the noise as well and signalled this to her brother. What could be making that noise? Ghosts don't walk! Or do they?

Then something moved the chair that was by Alan's desk. Samantha saw the movement and grabbed Alan's hand. She was terrified.

Thump! Something landed on the desk. It was going for the brownies!

Alan grabbed the flashlight from under the covers and pointed it straight at the desk and the brownies. Flipping on the switch, he and Samantha exclaimed in disbelief at the sight before them.

"Ronald!"

4

Ronald

Ronald stood like a deer caught in headlights. He did not move. Alan was still in shock but Samantha crawled out of the bed and went towards the elf.

"Ronald, what are you doing here? How did you get here?" she quietly asked him.

Her warm smile dispelled his fears and he sat down next to the brownies on the desk. He pulled his knees up to his chin and he gave Samantha a sad look. Tears trickled down his face. By this time Alan had joined them.

"Don't cry Ronald," he said kindly. 'It can't be that bad. Tell us what's wrong?"

Blowing on this tiny handkerchief, Ronald told them about all the trouble he got into because of the havoc Mark caused.

The Chief Elf sentenced Ronald to solitary confinement for two weeks. In addition he had to clean the work area everyday all by himself for another two weeks. Neither his parents nor his friends were speaking with him. He was very unhappy and so he ran away.

"But how did you find us?"

"By your smell Samantha," Ronald replied.
"My smell?" Samantha asked him a little surprised. "Do I smell bad?"

'No! No! Quite the opposite. You have a very sweet smell. Like a gardenia."

"I like gardenias," Samantha replied, "but I don't think I smell like one. Do I Alan?"

"He can't smell it," Ronald told them. "Only elves and other magical beings can smell it."

"Wow! That's amazing. So what does Alan smell like? Does he smell like a gardenia too?"

"No! Only magical beings have the smell."

"And I am?" Samantha asked completely astonished.

"You didn't know?" Ronald asked. He was the one surprised now.
"But how could Sam be magical and not me? And we are twins?" Alan asked.

"I don't know," Ronald replied. "Hopefully we will be able to find out."

Samantha was dizzy with the news. How could she be a magical creature? What was she? Did she have any special powers?

"Sam, imagine that? Maybe you could turn things into gold or fly. That would be cool. Or maybe breathe underwater. Or better yet, talk to animals."

Samantha was still stunned. She had never had any strange experiences before. Maybe in time she would learn who she was, if she was really a magical creature.

A nudge on her elbow brought her back to the present.
"Can I eat the brownie now?" Ronald asked her. "I haven't eaten all day."

"Of course you can." She broke the brownie into small pieces so it was easier for him to pick up.

As Ronald ate, Alan and Samantha looked at each other inquiringly. They shared the same thought, "How are they going to get Ronald back home to his own land?"

5

Adventure Time Again

The twins made a small bed for Ronald on the floor of Alan's room. In a split second he fell asleep and was snoring softly.

"What are we going to do with him?" Samantha asked her brother. They had gone over to Samantha's room so Ronald wouldn't hear them.
"I don't know. We will have to try to get him back to his home but I don't know how." Alan replied.

"We are not even sure if the Land of the Magical Shoes will ever reappear!" Samantha exclaimed in despair.

"We will just have to keep trying. We can't do anything about it right now so he will have to stay with us," Alan reasoned.

"But what about mom and dad? They won't understand."

"It will have to be our secret for now."

While Ronald slept peacefully, the twins had a restless night. The next day they decided to visit Mark. They hadn't seen him since the 'incident'. They thought that since it was his fault that Ronald ran away, he would have to help them get him back to his home.

When they arrived at Mark's house, he was very surprised to see them. He knew that they were very angry with him and he did not expect them to want to be friends anymore.

"Hello." He greeted them a little tentatively. "Is everything ok?"

"Hi Mark," Samantha said brightly and gave him a hug much to his amazement.

"Does that mean you are not mad at me anymore?" he asked, looking from Samantha to Alan.

"No, we are not mad anymore," Alan replied clapping him on the back. "It could have happened to anyone of us. We just have to be more careful next time."
They joked around for a few minutes like old times and then Alan got serious. "We actually have a little problem from that incident."

"A problem?" Mark asked

"Yes." He pulled Ronald out of his pocket where he was hiding.

Mark gasped. "How did he get here?" He bent to get a closer look at Ronald.

"Don't come close to me!" Ronald yelled at him which in his little elf voice came out more like a loud squeak. "You got me in plenty trouble you…you….you oaf!"

"I am sorry Ronald. Really I am."

Ronald continued to quarrel with Mark and wave his little elf finger at him for a few more minutes. When he settled down in Alan's palm, the twins explained to Mark how they discovered him and what had happened to him after they left the cave that day.

Mark felt badly. He could not even look at Ronald. It was all his fault that the elf was punished and had to run away from his home.

"So what are we going to do?" he asked Alan and Samantha. "We have to try to get him back to his home."

"Yes, but we don't know how," Samantha replied.

"Let's just go back to the cave and see what happens. That's the only thing we could do now. The answer has to be in the cave."

"Are we going back to the cave?" Ronald asked.

"Yes but we are not sure it will be your home this time."

"That's ok," he said with a big smile. "We're going on an adventure. I like adventures."

With that they set off to the cave. They hoped that the Land of the Magical Shoes would still be there but if not, they were ready for another adventure.

6

Toys, Toys Everywhere

Battery powered robots, cars and trucks moved helter skelter across the floor. Remote controlled helicopters and airplanes whizzed overhead while the sirens of the fire trucks filled the air. It was a kid's dreamland. A giant toy store!

The children walked into the toy store with their jaws dropped. Never before had they seen so many toys and so life-like.

"Oh my!" exclaimed Samantha. "Look at all those Raggedy dolls."
"And the G. I. Joes!" exclaimed Mark as he went racing towards the soldiers.

Ronald, who was peeping out from Alan's pocket, jumped to the ground and ran towards a model set of the fairytale, The Elves and the Shoemaker.

"Look at these elves! They look just like me."

The children followed him. The 'model' elves did look like Ronald. Alan picked him up and placed him on the shelf with the elves. Leaving him there they went to explore the rest of the store.

Suddenly, Ronald heard a voice behind him. "Hello."

He was not expecting to find anyone else in the toy store and jumped in fright.

"Don't be afraid. We mean you no harm."

As Ronald turned around, he saw and old, bald-headed man and an equally frail but motherly-looking woman.

"Did you say something?" he asked the couple not really expecting an answer.

"Yes. It was me," the old man replied shuffling towards him. "I have never seen you before. You are not one of the elves who help me."

"These elves are yours?" Ronald asked.

"No. Of course we are not his!" the closest elf replied as the others seem to come to life as well.

"I do not own them," the old man replied. "I am a shoemaker and they help me make shoes to sell so that I could buy food for my family."

"What is your name?" asked the shoemaker's wife.

"My name is Ronald."

"And where do you come from?" asked the shoemaker elf. "Where is your home?"

"I come from the Land of Magical Shoes."

"Never heard of there before," the shoemaker said shaking his head. "How did you come to be here?"

Ronald then told the shoemaker, his wife and the elves the sad story of how he got into trouble with the Chief Elf and why he ran away.

"That's terrible." The shoemaker's wife tried to comfort the sniffling elf. "You must miss your home."
"I do but I am afraid to go back. They will just punish me again," said the dejected elf.

"I am sure they will be very happy to have you back. They must be worried about you." The motherly old woman hugged Ronald trying to comfort him.

"Are you here by yourself?" one of the shoemaker's elves asked him.

"I am here with my friends," Ronald told them pointing upwards to Alan, Samantha and Mark who were now peering down at them.

"Oh dear," the shoemaker's wife jumped back in fright. "You are very big."

"Don't be frightened," Ronald assured them while he made the introductions.

"Do you have any idea how we can get Ronald back to his homeland?" Alan asked.

The shoemaker scratched his head thoughtfully. "We have always known that there are other lands out there but we don't know how to get to them."

"Maybe you could talk to the old wizard, Glaucis. He is very wise," said the elf and the others nodded in agreement.

"Where can we find this Glaucis?" Mark asked.

"Look for him in the mystical section with the wizards and warlocks. He should be next to Merlin."

Ronald thanked the shoemaker, his wife and the elves. Alan lowered his hand and Ronald jumped into his palm. They were off to find Glaucis.

It was easy to find the mystical section. There were bubbling cauldrons spewing smoke of every imaginable colour. At the same time young wizards and witches were trying out their new spells which were going horribly wrong. The sounds of crows squawking and the bats flying filled the air above them.

"Look! There is Merlin!" Samantha exclaimed pointing to the second shelf in the aisle.

He was sitting behind his desk stroking his long beard with a gentle smile on his face.

"Wow!" exclaimed Mark. "I never thought I would see Merlin in real."

"Come on! Let's find Glaucis." Ronald rushed them. "Let's see if he can help me get home."

"What's all the rush Ronald? Didn't you run away from home?" Mark asked.

"Yes, but I miss them," Ronald replied, a tear trickling down his cheek.

"Don't worry. We will get you home." Samantha comforted the little elf by hugging him.

"Look there! I think that is Glaucis," said Mark pointing to a skinny, bald-headed wizard with long, grey beard.

"Put me on the shelf. Let me talk to him," Ronald said to Alan.

Ronald made his way to Glaucis who was sitting on a large stone throne. As he got nearer the two wolves that were sitting at the wizard's feet perked their ears up and let out a low growl.

"It's ok boys," the wizard reassured them and Ronald appeared.

"Ah..ah...are they going to attack me?" Ronald asked glancing at the wolves that were bigger than he.

"Only if you try to attack me," said the old wizard stroking his beard. A large white owl flew through the air and landed comfortably on the back of the chair.

"I haven't seen you in here before. Nor have I seen your friends." Glaucis looked up and smiled at the children. "In fact I have never seen children before."

"How do you know we are children?" Samantha asked.

"After being alive for over 500 years, you learn many things."
"You are 500 years old! Wow!" Mark exclaimed.

"So what are you children and an elf doing here?"

Alan and Mark then took turns telling Glaucis about their magic cave, their adventures and how they came to find Ronald in their home.

The wizard looked at Mark with a stern eye. "That was not a nice thing to do to the elves."

"I know. I am sorry. I don't know what came over me."

"Magic can be a dangerous thing," Glaucis cautioned them. "You have to be very careful when dealing with it. It can make a good person go very bad."

"I know," Mark said hanging his head in shame.

"So how can I help you children and elf?"

"We are trying to find a way to get Ronald back home but since the cave keeps changing we don't know how to locate his land," Samantha explained.

The old wizard looked intently at Samantha. "You should be able to find his land easily. You have the scent of a Jaedan."

"A Jaedan? What's that?"

"A Jaedan my dear is a very powerful witch," Glaucis told them.

"A witch?" Samantha asked with a look of disgust on her face. "Witches are bad! I don't want to be a witch!"

Glaucis laughed. "You children read too many fairy tales. Not all witches are evil. There are good ones."

"Really?" Mark and Alan asked in unison.

"Yes. Everything in this world has an opposite. Hot and cold, day and night, happiness and sadness so you have evil witches and you have good witches. A Jaeden is a good witch."

"So what powers do I have? I never noticed anything before."

"You have the powers to control space."

"Space? How could I control space? There is nothing in space." Samantha said bewildered.

"Exactly. There is nothing there so you could make things appear in that nothingness."

"Things like what?" Mark asked.

The old wizard settled back in his chair. "Why do you think the magic cave showed itself to you and no one else?"

"Hmmm...I don't know. We thought we were just lucky enough to find it."

"Luck had nothing to do with it. Somehow Samantha made the cave appear."

"Wow! Sam, that's cool," Alan told his sister.

And then something struck them both at the same time. "If Sam is a witch and she is my twin sister, does that mean I have magical powers too?"

Glaucis scratched his beard. "Possibly. If you are really brother and sister."

7

Questions

When the children left the toy store and headed home, they had more questions than answers.

Glaucis told them that because Samantha was a Jaeden, she could command the Land of Magical Shoes to appear again. At least they might be able to reunite Ronald with his family but how did Samantha become a Jaeden? Was Alan a magical creature too?

They walked home in silence; too many thoughts were swirling in their minds.

"Are you kids ok?" their mother asked them as they sat down to dinner that night. She had prepared one of their favourite meals but they were just picking at it.

"It's so strange that you are so quiet," their father remarked. "Did something happen today?"

"No! Nothing happened!"

Their mom and dad looked at each other. Something was definitely up but they didn't press any further and so dinner continued in silence once more.

"Mom?" Samantha asked after a fifteen-minute silence.

Alan dropped his fork with a 'clang' and looked at his sister. He shook his head from left to right but Samantha did not pay him any heed.
"What is it, Sam?" her mom asked.

"Is Alan my real brother?" she blurted out.

"What?" It was now their parents' turn to be shocked.

"Of course he is. You are twins. What do you mean by that question? Did someone say something to you?" Anya asked while looking at her husband puzzled.

"No one said anything to us mom," Alan reassured his mother. "Sam is just being silly like a girl." He gave his sister a stern look.

"I just wanted to make sure because Alan is so ugly and I am so pretty," she added trying to make light of the situation.

The entire family laughed and the mood lightened as they finished their dinner.

"Are you crazy, Sam? How could you ask mom something like that?" Alan scolded his sister as they went upstairs to get ready for bed.

"I just wanted to know where my magical powers came from?"

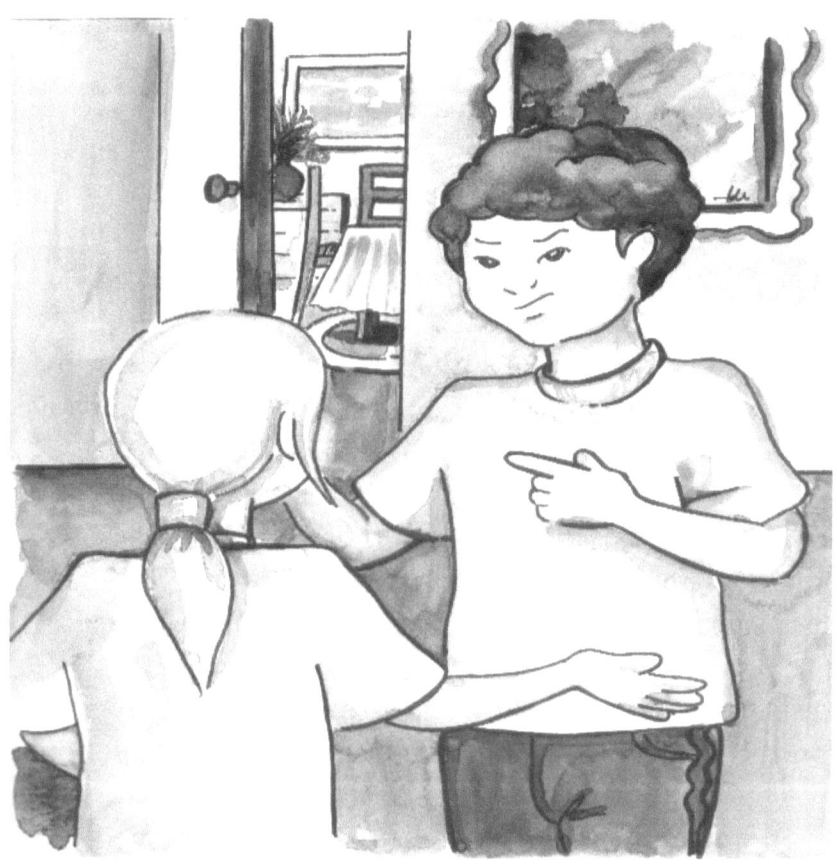

"I know but wouldn't mom and dad get suspicious? We will find out on our own."

"Don't forget you have to help me get home," Ronald reminded them. He was sitting on Alan's desk nibbling on a blueberry muffin that they had smuggled upstairs for him.

"Of course we won't forget. We will try, starting tomorrow."

8

We're not alone

The children were up at the crack of dawn and Mark soon joined them. With Ronald safely tucked away in Alan's pocket, they made their way to their beloved cave.

"I wonder what I have to do to make a land appear," Samantha commented.

"Wave your magic wand I suppose," Mark suggested.

"I don't have a magic wand, Mark."
"Oh right. Well. Just wish for it to appear and see what happens."

When they reached the cave, Samantha placed her hands on the rock and closed her eyes. The boys stood by and watched. They had no idea what she was supposed to do so they hoped for the best.

After a few minutes, they heard a low rumble coming from inside the cave.

"What's that?" Samantha asked stepping back from the rock.

"I guess it's the land you wished for. Let's go in and see."

"Yeah! It's time to go home!" Ronald exclaimed hanging out of Alan's pocket.

The children raced into the cave eager to find the Land of Magical Shoes. The sight that greeted them made their faces fall in disappointment.

"This is not my home," Ronald said as he sat heavily on the ground, a tear trickling down his cheek.

"I don't know what happened." Samantha tried to comfort him once again. "Maybe I don't know how to use my powers yet."

"Don't worry Ronald. We will get you home somehow," Mark said trying to cheer up the elf.

"Well since we are here let's find out what exactly is in this place."

The children and Ronald moved further into this new land. Stretching before them was a hard, grey and barren landscape.
"There are no trees or grasses."

"Or animals. I don't hear any sounds."

"Or see any people. What place is this?"

In the distance they could see rock formations rising high into the air.

"I wonder which part of the world this is? I have never seen any place like this on television or in books," Alan remarked.

"This is so weird. Doesn't even feel like we're on Earth anymore. The atmosphere feels....strange."

They continued to explore this strange place but did so cautiously, wary of anything that might spring at them.

"What's that over there? At the top of that rock?" Alan asked pointing to something waving in the air.

"I don't know but let's go and find out!" Mark exclaimed running off with Alan, Samantha and Ronald racing after him. They did not want to get separated in this strange place.

"It looks like a flag," Mark yelled to them.

As they got closer they could make out the type of flag very easily. "It's an American flag!" Alan exclaimed.

"But what is an American flag doing here? In the middle of nowhere," Samantha asked. "There doesn't seem to be anyone living here."

The children looked at each other puzzled. Why would an American flag be the only thing on the vast, barren landscape?

Suddenly Samantha broke the silence. "I know where we are!"

"Where?" Alan and Mark asked in unison.
"We're on the moon!"

Everyone looked at her stunned. How did they get to the moon?

"I probably was not concentrating very hard or not doing it right and we ended up here."

"The moon? Wow! Are you sure?"

"Yes. I saw a documentary on television. An American astronaut was the first human to land on the moon and he planted his country's flag."

'So you mean Earth is somewhere out there?" Mark asked pointing to the sky.

The children and Ronald looked up in awe at the sky. This was unlike anything they could have ever imagined.

Suddenly out of the corner of his eye, Ronald noticed a movement to his right. He tugged on Samantha's shirt and pointed in the direction of the movement. Four small, greyish, two-legged creatures were looking at them intently.

Their hands and feet were disproportionately large for their bodies and their bright eyes peered out of their small heads.

"There *are* creatures here!" Mark exclaimed

"Yes but nothing we have ever seen. What are they?" Samantha asked in a quivering voice.

The creatures did not come towards the children but just stood there looking at them.

"Do you think we should run?" Samantha asked.
"I don't think they mean to hurt us. If they wanted to they would have attacked us already," Alan told them.

"Maybe we should inch closer and see if they would communicate with us."

At Mark's suggestion the three inched closer to the aliens. For every step that they took towards them, the aliens came a little closer but they never made the first move.

Soon the children were face to face with the creatures. Ronald stuck his head out of Alan's pocket. He let out a small shriek and ducked back in once more.

"Hello." Samantha ventured after they stood in silence for a few minutes.

The four aliens looked at one another and then at the children.

"Hello," the tallest one said.

The children were stunned.

"You speak English?" Samantha asked.

"Yes. We speak all languages. We heard you speak when you first appeared and were able to learn your language," the tallest one replied. He seemed to be the leader of the group.

"You learned our language in a few minutes?" Alan asked.

"Yes. Our brains are highly evolved. If we lived on your planet, you would call us prodigies."

"You know where we come from?" Samantha asked even more intrigued.
"Yes. You come from Earth. We know about every species that lives on all the planets."

"Are there persons living on all the planets?" Mark asked. This was just getting weirder and weirder.

"Yes. Of course. Did you think that only Earth was inhabited?" The four aliens made a throaty sound that could have been a laugh.

"Actually yes. That's what we thought."

"No! There is life form on all the planets, earthlings. We are called Selenians. Life forms on Mars are Martians, on Venus they are Venusians and Saturn are Satarians."

Feeling no fear of the Selenians, the children continued to talk to them about their home planet. The leader, Kubuk, invited them to their home. He promised to return them to this same spot when their visit was over.

The children followed their new friends across the barren wilderness. They could not see any houses or buildings so they had no idea where Kubuk and his family lived.

Soon they arrived at a rock that resembled the one that blocked the entrance to their cave.

"I wonder if that is just a coincidence," Samantha remarked to Alan as they stopped at the rock.

Kubuk placed his hand on the rock and it easily slid away revealing a passage leading downwards. The children followed him with the other Salenians following.

The passage opened up into a well-lit, warm and cosy room. The light, however, did not come from bulbs. They came from glowing sticks that were placed strategically around the room.

"What are those?" Alan asked intrigued by the glowing sticks.

"They are made from lava rocks which make up our planet. It gives off both heat and light so very, as you say it on Earth, economical."

The sparse furniture in the room was made out of rocks found on the planet. Although hard it was quite comfortable.

As they sat down around the table, Kubuk poured them a wonderful tasting clear liquid. It was so refreshing that they all asked for more.

"What is this?" Alan asked.

"Water."

"Water? I never tasted water like this."

"Because this is pure water from our springs. It is not contaminated like yours. There are no chemicals or garbage in it. See how good your water could taste if earthlings stop dumping unclean items in it?"

"This definitely tastes delicious. I could drink this all day. It tastes better than juice and soda," Mark replied.

"When we go back home we will tell everyone how good clean water tastes. Maybe they will stop dumping garbage in the rivers and drains," Samantha told Kubuk.

"It's a good start. Thank you, Samantha."

"If you Selenians are so evolved, how come you don't have any television sets or video games?" Mark asked.

"Mark, having those things doesn't make you evolved. They are good for a little entertainment but you earthlings spend too much time on them. That's not good for the brain."

"It's not?" asked Mark and Alan together.

"No. It's not. Do you have to think a lot when you play your games or watch television?"

"Not really."

"And because of that you are not using your brain and soon the cells will start to die. We are highly evolved because we spend time writing stories, reading, drawing and exploring."

"Well we are going to try to do more of those things when we get home too," Samantha informed him.

"Very good. You are very bright Samantha."
After spending some more time with the Selenians, Kubuk walked them to the place where he met them. From here they could find their way back to the cave entrance.

"Goodbye my new friends," Kubuk said to them as he pressed his palm to his head and then to theirs. This was the Selenian way of saying farewell.

"Goodbye Kubuk," they told him hugging him in return.

"Take care and maybe one day we will come and visit you on Earth."

9

Mysterious Ring

After their out of space adventure, the twins and Mark cut down on the amount of television they watched and the video games that they played. Since these things were foreign to Ronald, he spent his days polishing and mending everyone's shoes and scaring Snoopy.

Samantha spent many hours at the local library researching magical creatures, especially Jaedens. At first it was hard to find information but when she did, she realized that Jaedens were actually very popular in the magical world.

She read all the books that she could find on the subject until she found the one thing she was really looking for.

How Jaedens Get Their Power

All Jaedens are born wearing a ring made out of gold mined from the deep recesses of the planet Shani. The ring is decorated with the precious stones, diamond and tanzanite in a circular pattern. It channels the Jaeden's thoughts to fill the space with what they desire. When the Jaeden dies the ring self-destructs.

Samantha leaned back on her chair. She searched her brain to remember if she had ever seen a ring like this at home but she couldn't recall. She would have to do some searching on her own, she said to herself.

She closed her books, returned them to the librarian and went home. Alan, Mark and Ronald were playing scrabble in Alan's room. Samantha did not bother to tell them she was home but went straight to her mother's room. Luckily Mrs. Harris was out running errands.

She checked through all the jewelry boxes but found nothing resembling the Jaeden ring. Next she searched the chest of drawers and the side table drawers but nothing. Glancing around the room, she wondered where else her mother could have hidden the ring, if it existed.

She wandered around the room a couple of times. It suddenly hit her. There was a box on the top shelf in her mother's closet that they were forbidden to even touch.

She gently pushed the closet door open and climbed on the lower shelves. She reached the top and found the forbidden box. Slowly opening the lid she peered inside. She gingerly balanced herself, pulled out the small velvet box that was inside and opened it!

She was astonished and almost fell off her precarious perch. Nestled inside the velvet box was her Jaeden ring!

"Oh my!" she exclaimed.

She gently removed the ring from the box and slipped it on the ring finger of her right hand. It fit perfectly. The sapphires let out a warm glow and then went out. The ring had recognized its owner.

She rushed to show the boys her discovery. Alan and Mark were still playing Scrabble and Ronald was playing with the scrabble squares that were half his size.

Looking up from their game they saw her excited look but she quickly silenced them with a finger on her lips.

She stretched out her hand and she showed them the Jaeden ring!

"That's a pretty ring." Mark said. "Where did you get it?"

"I hope you didn't take that from mom's jewelry box! She will be very angry," Alan told her.

"Well….I kinda did."

"What!" Alan exclaimed.

"Shush Alan. Wait till you hear my story."

Samantha then relayed to them her discovery in the library and then where she found the ring in her mother's closet.

"Are you sure that is *the* ring?" Mark asked excitedly.

"Well there is only one way to find out." Samantha said.

"Yippee! Yippee!" Ronald jumped up and down. "I am going home."

They raced to the cave excited to see if the ring would really work and the Land of Magical Shoes would reappear.

Once more Samantha placed her hand on the rock and thought about the Land of Magical Shoes. As she continued to focus her thoughts, the ring glowed brighter and brighter. Soon it was so bright they could not look directly at it. Suddenly it went out.

"Is that it?" Alan asked.

"Come on! Come on! Let's go in." Ronald ran ahead of them, eager to go home.

There, laid out in front of them, was the Land of the Magical Shoes!

"Woohoo! It worked!"

"I'm home! I'm home!" Ronald left them and ran towards the other elves.

The twins followed him, not sure what sort of homecoming he would get. Mark stayed close to the mouth of the cave. He was the one who had caused all the trouble in the first place and was very uncomfortable being here.

As Ronald ran towards the other elves, all work stopped and the place became silent. Suddenly two older elves came running towards him.
"Mom! Dad!" Ronald said, racing into their open arms.

"Son!" Tears were streaming down their faces. They were elated to have him back safely.

Soon the other elves gathered around them welcoming Ronald back home. It seemed as though all was forgiven.

"Thank you so much for bringing my son home," Ronald's mother said.

"You're welcome," Samantha told her, kneeling down to hug the little elf.

The elves started planning a welcome home party for Ronald and invited the children to stay. Although Mark was unwilling to stay, the elves assured him that he was forgiven. They stayed for many hours and enjoyed the elves' party. Ronald was definitely happy to be home and so were they.

10

Sea Creatures

"Did you put back the ring?" Alan asked Samantha when they returned home.

"No. It's my ring. I'm keeping it."

"But if mom finds out that it is missing, we will be in big trouble."

"I really don't want mom to get angry with me," said Samantha who loved her mom a lot and hated to see her angry.

"Then put it back, Sam."

"But then we won't be able to pick the places we want to go."

"It will just be a surprise and it will be more fun that way. We know where the ring is if you ever need it again," Alan reasoned with his sister.

"True."

Alan helped his sister return the ring safely to its velvet box before they went to bed. He was very happy that they were able to return Ronald to his family. He was even more excited that the three of them would be heading to another adventure the following day.

Alan was right, Samantha thought as she drifted off to sleep. It's more exciting when it's a surprise.
The next day dawned bright and sunny. It was definitely not a day to stay indoors. The smell of frying sausages made the twins jump out of bed, get dressed and rush downstairs. Much to their delight Mark was already there gobbling down his breakfast.

"I guess you guys are not staying inside today," their mother commented.

"No. It's too nice outside. We're going to the cave."

"I have to go with you to that cave sometime. You guys spend a lot of time there. What's so interesting about it?"

The children looked at each other.

"There is nothing really interesting. It's just a regular cave with bats and other creepy insects," Alan replied knowing that his mother detested bats.

"OK. Maybe some time when there are no bats then."

"That was close," Mark said when they had finished breakfast and went outside.

"Yes but I don't think she will ask to go again."

"Good! Let's go!" Mark exclaimed as he ran ahead of the twins.

Since they had decided they wanted to be surprised by the cave, they entered cautiously.

Before them stretched a long expanse of beach. The crystal clear water gently lapped the shore that was lined with tall coconut trees. The sky was cloudless, the sun was warm and the breeze was refreshing.
"I like this place," Samantha commented.

"Me too! It seems so peaceful," said Alan.

"Come on. Let's go for a swim," Mark said pulling off his t-shirt and heading for the water.

Within seconds the twins joined him, splashing and swimming and having great fun.

Suddenly Samantha shrieked.

"What happened Sam?" Mark asked stopping midway from splashing water on Alan.

"Something nibbled my toes."

All three dived below the water and what a sight met their eyes. Five huge turtles were swimming around them.

"Did you see that!" Samantha exclaimed as they resurfaced.

"They are huge! Almost as big as a pony!" Alan exclaimed excitedly.

"They don't seem dangerous though," Mark commented.

He felt something nudging his elbow. When he turned around, he was staring straight into the face of one of the turtles.

"Hello."

"You could talk?" Mark asked the turtle in disbelief.

"Yes. We can speak," the turtle replied gently.

By this time, the other four turtles had surfaced around them.

"Why don't you hold on to our shells so you don't have to tread water so much?"

"That won't hurt you?" Samantha asked.

"No. Our shells are very hard and strong. We won't even feel it."

"So who are you guys?" Alan asked the largest turtle. "I have never seen a turtle so big before."

"We are leatherback turtles."

"Do you live in the water all the time? Or do you come up on the land as well?" Mark asked getting a better grip on the turtle's shell.

"We live in the water in the deep ocean."

"Really? So what are you doing so close to shore?" Samantha asked.

"We come on shore to lay our eggs once a year. Only the females come up."

"So you are all girls?" Samantha asked looking around her at the huge animals.

The turtles let out a small chuckle. "Yes, my dear, we are all girls."

"Hey are any of you ready to go to shore? I think I am ready to lay my eggs," one of the smaller turtles said.

"I am ready too," another replied. "Carrying around these eggs is making me very tired. It would be good to get rid of the extra weight."

"Well, you two go ahead. You can take the children with you. I am sure they won't mind standing guard."

"Why do you have to have a guard when you're laying your eggs?" Alan asked. They were swimming to shore with the two turtles who were ready to lay.

"It's a very long, tiring process and when we are on shore we move very slowly. Sometimes when humans find us, they try to kill us for our meat."

"What? That's terrible."

"Why would they do that? Can't they see that you are laying your eggs and in a lot of pain."

"You children are very kind but many humans are cruel. Turtle meat is rare and fetches a lot of money so they try to kill us when we are vulnerable."

"Don't worry!" Mark assured them as they walked out of the shallow and onto the shore. "We will protect you."

The children were out of the water first. However, the turtles were moving a lot slower than when they were in the water.

"You guys really do move a lot slower on land," Alan commented as the turtles crawled across the sand.

"Yes! It is so much nicer in the ocean. I don't know how you humans can stay on land so much."

The children walked slowly at the sides of the two turtles until they found a suitable spot to lay their eggs.

"Are you going to make a nest for the eggs?" Samantha asked.

"Yes. We dig a hole in the sand with our back flippers and we lay the eggs in there."

"Don't stand too close," the other turtle warned them. "Or else you will get hit with the sand."

As the children watched, the turtles, using their powerful back flippers, dug a deep hole into which they laid their eggs. Then for the next hour the two mother turtles covered their nests. This time they used both their front and back flippers to move the sand.

Ever so often the turtle stopped and let out a deep breath.

"You must be so tired," Samantha commented to the one close to her.

"Yes. It is a long process to cover the eggs but we have to do it to ensure that they are not found."

An hour later the turtles were ready to return to the ocean.

"Do you come back when the eggs hatch?"

"No. The hatchlings run to the ocean and swim out to sea. We will return next year to lay more eggs."

The children accompanied the exhausted turtles to the water's edge. It was a long walk for them.
"Goodbye children. Maybe we will see you again next year."
With a small wave of their flippers, they disappeared into the waves and swam out to sea.

"That was very interesting," Alan commented as they watched the turtles go.

"Yes! Talking turtles! And we learnt so much."

"Who wants to go for another swim? Maybe we will meet some more talking creatures."

With that they dashed into the water again.

11

The Princess and the Witch

With the holidays slowly coming to an end, the children wanted to spend as much time as possible in the cave. However their mother had different plans for them. There were new school books, uniforms and supplies to be bought.

They knew there was no sense arguing with her so they accompanied her on her errands.

"I don't know why you two are so angry. The cave is not going anywhere," she said to them as they drove to the bookstore.

They just looked at her glumly. She will never understand, they thought.

"Ok. Here is the deal," she said trying to cheer them up. "Let's split up the tasks. I will get the textbooks and you guys pick out your supplies. That way we will get it done faster and you can go to your cave."

"Ok. Deal mom. Now can you drive a little faster?"

The twins wasted little time in picking out their new supplies for school. Luckily for them the bookstore was not crowded and Anya was able to purchase all their school books in record time.

When they got back home, Alan and Samantha flew out of the car.

"Hold on!" Anya shouted at them. "Come back here! Where do you think you are going in such a hurry?"

"But mom, you said we could go to the cave."

"Yes but don't you think you should help me unpack the car first?" She paused. "Sometimes I wish that cave would just disappear."

The children looked at her horrified. How could she say such a thing? Alan asked himself.

"Sorry. I didn't mean that. Just wished you guys would spend more time at home."

"Well since you're letting us go to the cave today, we could spend tomorrow at home with you," Alan said.

"But not doing errands," Samantha commented. "Doing fun stuff."
"Ok. Deal," Anya smiled at her kids. They were growing up too fast, she said to herself.

They hastily unpacked the car and raced off to find Mark who was at home and bored.

"Finally! I thought you guys would never come back," he told them as they ran towards the cave.

"Woohoo! Another adventure!" Alan exclaimed as they ran into the cave.

The sight that greeted them brought puzzled looks to their faces. Stretching as far as they could see was a forest of dark green trees. The place was silent.

"This is eerie. What is this place?"

"I don't know but let's see if we could figure it out."
The children ventured into the dark, cool forest. The tops of the trees were so close that the sunlight could not get through.

"I don't think this is a good idea guys," Samantha said. "This doesn't feel like a happy place. Something is wrong."

"Let's go a little further."

After walking for a further ten minutes the trees thinned out.

"There's something up ahead. I see something moving," said Mark who was in the lead.

The children hid behind a tree and cautiously peered out into the clearing. What they saw made them gasp. In the middle of the clearing stood a small house that was made out of a giant mushroom. Seven dwarves were standing in front of the house.
"It's the seven dwarves!" Samantha exclaimed.

"Yes. We could see that but who is that on the ground in front of them?"

Lying on the ground was a beautiful girl. Her skin was white as snow and her hair was raven black.

"It's Snow White!"

The dwarves looked up suddenly, realizing that they were not alone. As the children stepped into the open, they huddled together on one side of the body.

"We didn't kill her. Please don't harm us. We didn't kill her," the youngest dwarf cried out. He looked no older than twelve.

"We won't harm you," Samantha said kindly, moving towards them.
"What happened?" Mark asked, kneeling in front of the body.

"Someone tried to poison her. She bit into that apple there and then fell down and died," said a teary-eyed dwarf.

The other dwarves, realizing that the children were not going to harm them, huddled around Snow White once more.

"Who would try to kill such a beautiful girl?"

"Her evil stepmother who is a witch."

Suddenly they heard loud sounds of persons and animals crashing through the forest.

"Hurry! Let's get her inside! They're coming for her!"

The dwarves gently picked up Snow White's body and carried her inside their little cottage.

"Come on!" a chubby dwarf yelled to us from the front door.

"We can't fit in there. It's too small." Alan shouted back over the din of the oncoming animals.

"Yes you can! Come on!"

The children looked at one another apprehensively. There was no way they could fit into such a small house. The sound of approaching voices, however, hurried them inside.

The little door slammed behind them and a dwarf placed a heavy wooden bar across it. To their amazement, the little cottage seemed to grow when they stepped inside. They could actually stand upright.

The dwarves gathered around the body of Snow White which was laid on the sofa. She looked even more beautiful in the cottage's dim light.

"I can't believe she is gone," sobbed one of the dwarves.

"She was so beautiful and kind."

"Why did her stepmother kill her?" Samantha asked. She could never imagine her mother wanting to kill her.

"Because the Prince was in love with her and the evil stepmother wanted him to marry one of her hideous daughters."

"Oh my!"

They were interrupted by a loud bang on the front door.

"I know you have the wretched girl in there!" the witch wailed. "Give her body to me!"

"No! We will not!" shouted one of the elder dwarves.

"I want her body! Give her to me!" She banged what sounded like a staff on the door. "If you don't I will come in to get her. You know you can't stop me." She then let out a raucous laugh that chilled the children to their bones.

"What are we going to do?" the grand-motherly looking dwarf asked.

"They can't get us in here. The magic will protect us."

"Yes but we can't stay in here all the time. We will have to go out to get food."

"Maybe we could go out. She doesn't know us," Mark offered.

"No! She is so angry she will kill you too."

"But if Snow White is already dead why does she want the body?"

"She has to destroy it. If the Prince finds her and kisses her on her lips she will come back to life."

The witch rapped on the door again. "Give me the body, you foolish dwarves. Or else I will kill all of you."

The dwarves huddled together and the children watched helplessly. There was nothing they could do.
Suddenly the house started to shake. There was a loud howling outside.

"She is trying to blow the house down so she could get the body!"

"And she will kill us."

"I thought this house was magic?" Alan asked.

"Yes but not strong enough to withstand a powerful witch."

Then as suddenly as the wind started, it stopped.

"What happened?" one of the dwarves asked as he headed for the door.

"No! Don't go out there! It could be a trick."

Everyone listened intently to see if he or she could make out what was going on outside.

"Hold her!" they heard someone command.

"It's the Prince," one of the dwarves said.

"The Prince has come to save his beloved."

The dwarves and the children rushed outside. Several of the Prince's men were holding the witch. When the Prince saw the dwarves, he got off his white stallion and ran to them.

"Where is she? Where is my love?" he asked them.

"She is inside my Prince. Hurry and save her."

They all followed the Prince inside leaving his men to guard the witch. The Prince knelt next to Snow White. He took her pale hand into his and gently stroked her face. Slowly he planted a kiss upon her apple-red lips.

Everyone held his breath, hoping that Snow White would wake up. The minutes ticked by and then slowly her eyes fluttered open and she took a deep breath.

The children joined the dwarves in letting out loud shouts of joy. The Prince gathered Snow White into his arms and gently helped her stand up. His eyes were filled with tears.

Hand in hand they went outside. As soon as the witch saw that Snow White was alive, she started to scream at the top of her lungs. The voice was deafening and the children covered their ears to block out the sound.

"Take her away and shut her in the dungeons!" the Prince commanded.

The witch continued to scream as she was taken away but no one cared. The Prince got down on one knee in front of Snow White and took her hands in his.

"Snow White, I can't bear to lose you again. Will you marry me?"

"Yes. Of course. I love you more than life itself," she answered, choked with emotion.

A loud cheer went up from the crowd gathered which now included many deer, rabbits and birds.

"We are sorry your visit here was scary. Would you stay for the celebrations tonight?" the elder dwarf asked Alan.

"Yes. We would love too," Samantha answered.

That night the children partied with the Prince, Snow White, the dwarves and many others who loved their Prince and Snow White.

"What a nice party!" Mark said as they made their way to the entrance of the cave.

"Yes. It was," Alan replied.
"I hope one day I get married to a Prince," Samantha commented.

"Well as long as we have the magic cave, anything could happen."

Aarti Gosine started writing at the tender age of 8. Her short stories were first published in the Junior Express, a local publication for children.

Her love for writing children's stories has continued over the years as she now writes for the Kid's Page of the Northerly. She is also a creative writing tutor for 9 – 11 year olds.

Her first novel is The Magic Cave.

More Adventures In The Magic Cave is the sequel to The Magic Cave.

www.ingramcontent.com/pod-product-compliance
Lightning Source LLC
Chambersburg PA
CBHW020632130626
46552CB00003B/1186